ROMANCE PROMPTS
& BEATS WORKBOOK

to help you
write your romance novel

By
Lena Lacrosse & Adriana Gillander

GUILDED MONOCLE

Published by Guilded Monocle LLC

Written and Compiled by Lena Lacrosse and Adriana Gillander

Cover Design by Guilded Monocle

IBSN : 979-8-9908884-0-1

Guildedmonocle.com

AUTHOR'S NOTE

Hello dear reader and fellow writer,

First off, you should know that only after we embarked on this adventure - we realized our ideas of 'prompts' were different, so we tried to include both of our ideas (narrative and descriptive prompts). We've tried to compensate for how our thought patterns differ - Lena likes a clear question, while Adriana likes either to be completely open to possibilities or to follow a checklist. Thus, we purposefully repeat ourselves in different formats to accommodate divergent thought patterns.

Second, we have tried to make these romance prompts for a broader audience; to be more inclusive of different types of love and romance. Thus the names and pronouns vary but of course you can change any of them for your own style.

We (Lena and Adriana) present to you, with bated breath and hopeful approval, a book of guided prompts that will help you build your romance novel or novella. We hope it inspires lovely and amazing characters; pitiable, laughable and tear jerking scenes; and slays writer's block and side quests like the proverbial knight in shining armor, (or perhaps we should be more realistic and consider it their squire - simply poking a stick at those beasts or beats).

With great affection and gratitude,

Lena Lacrosse and Adriana Gillander

INTENTIONALLY LEFT

Blank

(please use this to doodle or take notes)

How to use this hybrid workbook/prompter:

Part 1: Outline General Romance Beats. We are by no means saying this is comprehensive of romance beats needed in your novel, but it is a start. We each like different writers' takes on the beats and their descriptions, and we urge you to use the ones that suit your story to craft your complete novel. But we all need a place to start and we hope this suffices. We then have a few places throughout the workbook to write a summary because things change as they develop.

Part 2: Playful Prompts (specific and narrative style) to explore your character, setting, and theme.

Part 3: Beat Prompts Each two-page spread contains one prompt on the left and an additional callout box on the lower right containing examples or help with the prompts. Since our neurodivergent brains work differently, we thought to include both- (although yes we definitely realize the typical creative right brain appears on the left, while the bullet pointed left brain appears on the right.)

Part 4: Troubleshooting - For when the words or thoughts just don't come, and you fear your muse is in hermit mode.
- Random diversions for when you get stuck
- Word list
- Scenario prompts

Part 5: Afterglow - Summary and congrats! Yay you did it! Here are a few summary pages. They have room for your personal summary, then space to craft your synopsis and blurb.

INTENTIONALLY LEFT

Blank

(please use this to doodle or take notes)

PART 1:

Outline of general romance beats and what that section should cover.

0   • **Who are your characters?**
- o Who are the main characters?
- o What type of relationship theme do they exhibit?
- o What drives them, what makes them tick?
- o What does their daily life look like?
- o What are they missing? What does your character lack, want, desire, need? Is their life stagnant? Chaotic?
- o What are their internal struggles that say NO to love?
- o What external forces may keep them from love?

1   • **Opening Scene/ Introduce Your Characters**
- o Include your hook
- o Hint at your trope
- o What do each of your main characters lack?

2   • **Inciting Incident**
- o Describe the moment things change. What sets the story in motion and leads to the meet cute?

3   • **Meet Cute**
- o What could go wrong? Or very, very right, when the lovers meet?
- o How do the two meet? How does the trajectory of their lives change?
- o Is there instant attraction? If so, introduce obstacle(s) to being together.
- o Or is there instant dislike? Do both refuse The relationship.What do they have in common?
- o Set them up to work towards a common goal. They should use their past experiences or values.

4   • 'It's a No' (Push away / Resist the connection)
   o One or both of the main characters try to resist their
     connection/attraction. One or both characters intend to
     follow the plans they had before meeting. Why can't it
     work out - is it internal or external (unloving or
     indifferent parents, disbelief in love, classist beliefs, live
     in different countries, speak different languages,
     different genders, etc.) What are they in denial about?
     What are the small things they notice? The attractions?
     What gets and keeps their attention on the other
     character?

5   • **Forced to work together**
   o **"UGH Fine"** —Thrown together - Our to-be loves/lovers
     are forced to be together for some reason. Their
     individual plans are thwarted or changed by being
     forced to be together.
   o **"OK Whatever"** - Common ground - They recognize that
     the challenge cannot be overcome/ goal not achieved
     unless they work together. They are growing closer but
     still fighting it. Internal battles are mounting. (Accept
     working together but do not accept their attraction.)

6   • **"Still a NO but..."**
   o Two Steps forward and one step back - We see them
     interacting with each other at different times in
     different situations, possibly a date(s), but the
     issue/thing that keeps them apart always becomes
     evident. This section and beat usually includes: growing
     attraction, restating why they 'can't' be together, and a
     few key scenes to build emotional knowledge, intimacy
     and sexual tension.

7 • "Maybe I was wrong," Character Shift
   ○ There is a change in the main character or characters that leads them to who they will be at the end. They start questioning their reasons things can't work.

8 • False High
   ○ It appears everything is going to work out perfectly, falling in love.
   ○ Admitting feelings - At least one admits feelings for the other (maybe out loud or internally).
   ○ Could be - Where they see that maybe there could really be something but ...
   ○ Doubt creeps in - The characters express their feelings and admit their doubts/ fears.

9 • The Shoe Drops
   ○ Something goes wrong to drive a wedge between them. There is a break in trust, miscommunication, or similar. Makes character(s) question - or nothing happens but previous doubts and insecurities arise. *Nothing worth it is ever easy.* What wedge is driven between them? How deep is it? How wide is the chasm?
   ○ How have the characters changed when their first fears of love/intimacy are proved right? In some respects? The larger the chasm, the deeper and more powerful the drama. What leads them to break up? The (almost) final straw?

10 • Hitting bottom / breakup/ ties severed
   ○ They seem like they will never get together. Everything is dramatic and everything is wrong. The external force that kept them together is over and the dropped shoe/wedge has made this relationship end (for now).

11 • **"What have I done?" Moment of realization**
  ○ The main character realizes they may have made a mistake. This is the memory montage of happy moments that challenges false beliefs.

12 • **"I choose you,"**
  ○ After the moment of realization, the main character chooses love over doubt and fear. What happens to make them do this? What are they willing to sacrifice? What internal demons do they strike down, root out? What decisions do they make to follow love and forsake their false beliefs?

13 • **Boom Box Moment**
  ○ Climax/Sacrifice/Grand gesture - Show the main character putting it all on the line. Actions speak louder than words. You must show them making a grand gesture to display overcoming internal and external conflicts and adversity. How do they show their love? Think grand love languages? How do they tell each other of their love and accept it?

14 • **Happily Ever After- Denouement**
  ○ Here is the Happy Ending we've been working towards. Show them together, happy and safe. Show how they have changed and make sure to resolve their internal and external conflicts fully. Make sure you fulfill expectations, close all arcs, explain all plot holes.

15 • **Epilogue**
  ○ Continue the denouement for a further story - Is there a wrench hurled into their world, or it can be 20 years on. Where is the happy couple now? Is another couple destined for the same happy fate?

Possible Tropes

Relationship Shift

(already know eachother)

- Friends to Lovers
- Exes to Lovers / 2nd chance
- Enemies to Lovers
- Neighbors to Lovers
- Forbidden Love
  - family's enemy
  - sibling's best friend
  - married love

Truth and Lies

- Fake relationship
- Blackmail
- Betrayal
- Mistaken Identity
- Different supernatural or Alien species
- Amnesia

Situational Change

- Single Parent
- Love Triangle
- Makeover
- Kidnapped

Job based tropes

- Nanny
- Military
- Royalty
- Medical
- Job/Promotion rival

Setting Change

- Forced proximity
- New to town (city/town switch)
- Vacation romance turns long term
- Escape from relationship
- Blind date
- Summer romance
- Meet at a Wedding

Fairy Tale

- Rags to Riches (Cinderella)
- Riches to Rags
- Status mismatch
- Cursed
- Faked death/ back from the dead
- Soulmates

It's complicated, be careful

(include trigger warnings for all readers but especially these)

- Healing from violent trauma
- Alpha/ bully
- Terminal - involves life threatening illness, grieving loss
- Lost/adopted child
- Rejection from coming out
- Revenge love
- Guardian/ward to love

Intentionally Left

Blank

(please use this to doodle or take notes)

PART 2:

Playful prompts

TO GET YOU IN
THE MOOD..

10+ Narrative prompts to get you started on a story, inspire themes or relationships to write about. You don't need to do all or any of them, but they are a good starting point. Please note: although the majority are cis-hetero romance pronouns and names, please alter as needed/desired. That said, we have also included some she/she, he/he, they/they, and combinations thereof, because LOVE IS LOVE!

CHARACTER PROMPT:

Lucifer and Lilith hated their names, or moreover they hated the reactions to them. People supposed so much based just on their meaning and history. But truly they were good, or at least they tried to be. That was until they were accused of stealing her Lady's jewels! But what really happened was...

CHARACTER PROMPT:

The best thing about being an agent was that no one, well, almost no one, knew her real name. Jazzie Midnight was a name that should have been reserved for the stage. Sitting alone at the _____ eating _____ reminded her of...

CHARACTER PROMPT:

Glenda was always thought to be good. Which made being bad all the more fun. Her favorite wreck of havoc was the time she _____, and Eddie had never forgotten it. This made their chance meeting at the _____ all the more awkward.

ACTIVITY SHEET 1:
NAMES, MEANINGS AND ASSOCIATIONS

Create a list of names:

Look up some names within the year your characters were born, baby names, or look up names and meanings. This could also be a list of what you wished you were named, or a list of people you've encountered—and would never name your children after, etc...

CHARACTER PROMPT:

Evan was quite the harsh critic but meeting Lady Elloise had softened him. Then she appeared in the local play. She was truly appalling at acting. What could be done but...

(Hint: What makes your character tick?)

CHARACTER PROMPT:

Harold was an accountant, no, not that sort, the traditional kind. He kept his tie as straight as his figures. That was until his hapless new temp stumbled onto his secret...

(Hint: What does their life look like? What are they hiding?)

CHARACTER PROMPT:

Deandra couldn't believe she'd actually done it! But now she had to tell Ari. What would they think?

(Hint: What bad habits does Deandra have? What fears?)

CHARACTER PROMPT:

In high school, Jenny had idolized Dan. He was athletic and smart and everything she thought she wanted. But after nine years, she found out she was wrong...

(Hint: What acts can Jenny not forgive and why?)

CHARACTER PROMPT:

Lui had been in the closet until they were 22, but a chance
meeting with Palmer changed everything...

(Hint: What are the words Lui has been longing to hear?)

CHARACTER PROMPT:

Finally after 10 years, Ahni was up for promotion, to full editor. They just had one more story to break, so why did it have to be about *her*? (*Hint: What does your character want?*)

Character Prompt:

Jo loved the quirky side of life, and collected _____. They never thought it would lead them to disaster or to love, depending on how you looked at it.

(Hint: What does your character lack? What are they looking for?)

CHARACTER PROMPT:

Darlene loved chocolate. Chocolate had never let her down, not like Mike. Her heart skipped a beat when Jenny walked into her shop that day and had been skipping ever since.

(Hint: How does what she 'wants' and what she 'needs' differ?)

CHARACTER PROMPT:

It was everything she had never dreamed of. She wasn't sure if she had been too afraid to aim this high, or she just hadn't known it was possible.

(Hint: What does your character lack?)

CHARACTER PROMPT:

"This is the pits," they said in unison. Then they both tried to speak at the same time, "This is all your fault!"

(Hint: What is the lowest point each can imagine?)

SETTING PROMPT:

It wasn't a dark and stormy night, in fact it was a beautiful day, the best ever!

(Hint: What would your character's perfect day look like? What scene inspires contentment? Include more than April 25.)

SETTING PROMPT:

"What a beautiful sunset/sunrise..."

(Hint: describe the scene from either a romantic or skeptical perspective. Are there amazing colors, perhaps due to dust in the air? Is it just after a storm? Are we at a beach, a bluff, a skyscraper?)

25

SETTING PROMPT:

Looking down at her feet, she was amazed at what she saw...
(Hint: What does the floor look like? Concrete, mosaics, black sand, or is she at the edge of a cliff and looking at the lapping waves?)

SETTING PROMPT:

That was definitely the best seat in the house. Alas, they were seated here...

(Hint: Are the couple at a concert? A restaurant? At home in front of the TV? On a cruise? What stops them from being where they wish they were? And how can they get there?)

SETTING PROMPT:

"I can't climb that hill again."

(Hint: describe the scene before the speaker. Are they exercising or training? Are they lost? Is it a big hill or a metaphorical one? Or is it more like a mountain but the speaker is from somewhere flat?)

SETTING PROMPT:

I want you to redesign my office. I want it to look _____.

(Where would your main character be 'productive'? What would they want to surround them if they won the lottery? Cleanliness or a Victorian library, or a cozy comfortable space?)

SETTING PROMPT:

"It was the most glorious sight he had ever seen. Even if he'd seen it 100 times."

What is the character's oasis or haven after a long or tragic day? What is something they may have taken for granted before?

ACTIVITY SHEET 2:
FIRST TAKE ON YOUR BOOK

(This is just a place to start, don't worry everything can change)

Romantic trope: (please circle one or fill-in)
Enemies to lovers, Friends to Lovers, Secret/Mistaken Identity,
Fake relationship, Love Triangle, Second Chance Romance.
Other_____

Point of View: (please circle one or fill-in)
First (I, we), Second (you), Third (he, she, they)
Specifically_____

Where:

When:

Character 1 Name:

Character 2 Name:

Thoughts and Notes:

INTENTIONALLY LEFT

Blank

(please use this to doodle or take notes)

PART 3

Beat Prompts

THE ACTION
YOU'RE
LOOKING FOR

We hope these help you to start writing your novel with character traits, drivers, actions and scenes that you can draw on later for your novel/novella. Some beats have more than one prompt.
When getting to know your characters - there are two pages per prompt - for character 1 and character 2.

BEAT PROMPT 0

Now that you have begun the journey with your chosen characters and the trope, let's get to know these characters better.

BEAT PROMPT 0.01: GET TO KNOW CHARACTER 1

Write something that your character is passionate about and why, include an event or person that ignited the passion.

Write something that your character is passionate about and why, include an event or person that ignited the passion.

Examples:

- <u>Career</u>: Doctor to help people after sick family member dies
- <u>Hobby</u>: Desserts/baking: because grandmother showed love that way
- <u>Role</u>: Parent or caretaker

GET TO KNOW CHARACTER 1:
BEAT PROMPT 0.02

Write about a secret indulgence your character has and why it is a secret. Is it divergent from the rest of their personality?

GET TO KNOW CHARACTER 2:
BEAT PROMPT 0.02

Write about a secret indulgence your character has and why it is a secret. Is it divergent from the rest of their personality?

Examples:
- Collector of clocks or taxidermy
- Addict
- Foodie
- Romantic
- Poet
- Air guitar performer
- Craft hoarder

GET TO KNOW CHARACTER 1:
BEAT PROMPT 0.03

Does your character have a "ride or die" friend/partner? It could be a platonic or romantic relationship. What have they done for each other to gain this title? If they don't have a "ride or die"/bestie, write about what they are looking for or why they don't think one exists.

GET TO KNOW CHARACTER 2:
BEAT PROMPT 0.03

Does your character have a "ride or die" friend/partner? It could be a platonic or romantic relationship? What have they done for each other to gain this title? If they don't have a "ride or die"/bestie, write about what they are looking for or why they don't think one exists.

Examples:
- Childhood friend
- Close cousin
- Partner turned bestie
- Former cell mate
- Colleague
- Neighbors
- Fraternity brother or Sorority sister

39

GET TO KNOW CHARACTER 1:
BEAT PROMPT 0.04

Write about your character's family life as a child and in the
present. Do their adult relationships mirror their childhood ones?
Write an incident that shows how they are similar or different.

GET TO KNOW CHARACTER 2: PROMPT BEAT 0.04

Write about your character's family life as a child and in the present. Are people in their adult relationships similar to their childhood ones? Write an incident that shows how they are similar or different.

Examples:
- Happy/unhappy
- Divorced/together
- Functional/codependent
- Melded/complex
- Orphaned/abandoned
- Absent parents
- Birth order
- Wealth/status

GET TO KNOW CHARACTER 1:
BEAT PROMPT 0.05

Write about a time when your character felt truly scared and/or helpless.

GET TO KNOW CHARACTER 2:
BEAT PROMPT 0.05

Write about a time when your character felt truly scared
and/or helpless.

Examples:
- Home alone
- Locked in
- Darkness
- Alien encounter
- Illness
- Natural disaster
- Car won't start
- Abandoned mansion

GET TO KNOW CHARACTER 1:
BEAT PROMPT 0.06

Describe an event in which your main character felt pure elation.

GET TO KNOW CHARACTER 2:
BEAT PROMPT 0.06

Describe an event in which your main character felt pure elation.

Examples:
- School or job success
- Witnessing a natural event (meteor shower, aurora borealis)
- Best meal
- Music/concert/art
- Travel adventure
- Sexual experience

45

GET TO KNOW CHARACTER 1:
BEAT PROMPT 0.07:

Who is your main character? Describe them physically, mentally, & emotionally. Does their personality differ between social and work situations? What makes them unique?

Describe them physically, mentally, & emotionally. Does their personality differ between social and work situations? What makes them unique?

Examples:
- Words they'd use to describe themselves in a job interview
- Their 5 year goals
- New Year's resolution
- Halloween costume: supermodel or mousy librarian

GET TO KNOW CHARACTER 1:
BEAT PROMPT 0.08

What drives them? What makes them tick?

What drives them? What makes them tick?

Examples:
- School or job focused
- Family
- Adrenaline junky
- Introvert
- Learning
- Exploring
- Money

GET TO KNOW CHARACTER 1: BEAT PROMPT 0.9

What does their daily life look like?

What does their daily life look like?

Examples:
- Vocation/Job Title
- Hobbies
- Siblings
- Friend group
- After work schedule
- Morning routine
- Daily commute - car, bus, metro, walk, work from home?

GET TO KNOW CHARACTER 1:
BEAT PROMPT 0.10

What are they missing? What does your character lack, want, desire, and/or need? Is their life stagnant? Chaotic?

Get to know Character 2:
Beat Prompt 0.10

What are they missing? What does your character lack, want, desire, need? Is their life stagnant? Chaotic?

Examples:
- Work driven, lacks personal life-feels lost
- Searching for soul mate
- Enjoys being single and doesn't think they are missing anything
- Connection
- Juggling too many things

GET TO KNOW CHARACTER 1:
BEAT PROMPT 0.11

What are their internal struggles? Why do they say NO to love?

GET TO KNOW CHARACTER 2:
BEAT PROMPT 0.11

What are their internal struggles? Do they believe in love? Why do they say NO to love?

Examples:
- Feel abandoned
- Heartbroken
- Lacks trust
- Financially unstable
- Family illness/ commitments
- Career oriented
- Tired

GET TO KNOW CHARACTER 1:
BEAT PROMPT 0.12

What are external forces that may also keep them from love?

What are external forces that may also keep them from love?

Examples:
- No time to date/love
- Status and access (rags to riches/ Cinderella)
- Overbearing parents
- Memory/ amnesia
- Family or work rivalry (Romeo and Juliet)
- Parenthood/children

INTENTIONALLY LEFT

Blank

(please use this to doodle or take notes)

My Book of Romance

NOVEL PLAN

*(please fill out before you begin to easily reference &
either keep you on track or change, feel free to reference or discard
your first instincts from pg. 31)*

Working Title:

Romantic trope:
☐ Enemies to lovers ☐ Friends to Lovers ☐ Fake relationship
☐ Secret/Mistaken Identity ☐ Love Triangle
☐ Second Chance Romance ☐ Other_____

Point of View: First (I, we), Second (you), Third (he, she, they),
(limited, ominiscient, objective).
Character 1:
Character 2:

Where:
When:
Character 1 name:
Character 2 name:

Blurb:
(100-200 words with: Hook, Characters, Tone, Genre, Conflict &
Stakes.)

BEAT PROMPT 1: INTRODUCE CHARACTERS 1 & 2

Opening scene with a hook.

What do each of your main characters lack?

BEAT PROMPT 1

Help:
- Introduce each character
- Include what they (actually) lack
- Include what they **think** they want
- Let us see a bit of their everyday lives
- Setup the conflict

BEAT PROMPT 2: INCITING INCIDENT

Describe the moment everything changes.

(Did someone lose their job? Get a promotion? Win the lottery? Inherit a house? Set up the challenge to love.)

BEAT PROMPT 2

Help:
- What event sets this story in motion?
- What has suddenly changed in one of their lives to make this day different?
- What leads them to the meet cute?

63

BEAT PROMPT 3: MEET CUTE

How do the two meet? What could go wrong? Or very, very right, when the lovers meet? How does the trajectory of their lives change?

Help:
- Is there instant attraction? If so introduce obstacle(s) to being together.
- Or is there instant dislike = both refuse relationship, but WHY should they be together?

BEAT PROMPT 4: "IT'S A NO" - PUSH AWAY/ RESIST THE CONNECTION

One or both of the main characters try to resist their connection/attraction. One or both characters intend to follow the plans they had before meeting.

(Why can't it work out? Is it internal or external? (Unloving or indifferent parents, disbelief in love, classist beliefs, live in different countries, speak different languages, work for rival companies, or different sexual orientations or attractions from past experiences.)

Help:

- What are they in denial about?
- What are the small things they notice?
- What attracts them to each other?
- What gets and keeps their attention on the other character?

Beat Prompt 5: Forced to Work Together

5. 1 "Ugh Fine"–Thrown Together

Our to be loves/lovers are forced to be together for some reason. Their individual plans are thwarted or changed by an external force so that now they must work together.

BEAT PROMPT 5.1

Help:
- What external forces pushed them together?
- How are they tolerating being stuck together?
- Are they trying to find a way out?
- What terms/timelines have they accepted?

69

BEAT PROMPT 5: FORCED TO WORK TOGETHER
5. 2 "OK WHATEVER"

Our characters find common ground. They recognize that the challenge cannot be overcome/ goal cannot be achieved unless they work together. They are growing closer but still fighting it. Internal battles are mounting. (They accept working together but do not yet accept their attraction.)

Help:
- What common ground do they have?
- Are they starting to respect the person?
- Are they still counting down to when they can go their separate ways?
- Have they found a way to work together?

BEAT PROMPT 6: "STILL A NO, BUT..."

Two Steps forward and one step back: We see them interacting with each other at different times in different situations, possibly on date(s), but the things keeping them apart always becomes evident. This beat usually includes: growing attraction, restating why they *can't* be together and a few key scenes to build emotional knowledge, intimacy, and sexual tension.

Help:

- When do they share these moments?
- Does banter or a shared secret confirm their connection?
- How does the reason they can't be together always emerge?

BEAT PROMPT 7: "MAYBE I WAS WRONG" CHARACTER SHIFT

There is a major shift in the perspective of the main character(s). This change leads the character to who they will be at the end. They start questioning their reasons things can't work.

Help:
- What ignites the change in the characters' perspectives?
- Do they make each other better people?
- Have they found a balance?
- Did they find a common enemy?

BEAT PROMPT 8: FALSE HIGH

8.1 ADMITTING FEELINGS

Appears everything is going to work out perfectly. Characters are falling in love and at least one admits feelings for the other (either outloud or internally).

BEAT PROMPT 8.1

Help:
- Have they let their guard down?
- Are they feeling confident? Insecure?
- Have the obstacles disappeared?
- If one hasn't admitted feelings does this cause tension?

77

BEAT PROMPT 8: FALSE HIGH

8.2 COULD BE...

Where the characters see that maybe there could really be
something between them, but...

BEAT PROMPT 8.2

Help:

- Are they starting to look past the thing keeping them apart?
- Are they making plans for their future?
- What is making one or both hesitate?
- What is the pivotal thought that signals change?

BEAT PROMPT 8: FALSE HIGH

BEAT PROMPT 8.3 DOUBT CREEPS IN...

The characters express their feelings to eachother and admit their doubts/ fears.

BEAT PROMPT 8.3

Help:
- Does admitting doubts or fears bring them together or push them apart?
- Will their fears be realized?
- Do they both feel the same way or is one insistent that they should be together.

81

BEAT PROMPT 9: THE SHOE DROPS

Something goes wrong/drives a wedge between them. There is a break in trust, miscommunication, or similar. Previous doubts, & insecurities arise. The deeper the chasm between them, the more powerful the drama. This is what leads them to break up.

Help:
- Does one or both characters feel betrayed?
- Has the other committed a "deal breaking" offense?
- Has their worst fear come to fruition?

Beat Prompt 10: Break up

The lovers seem like they will never get together. Everything is dramatic and everything is wrong. The external force that kept them together is over and the dropped shoe/wedge has made this relationship end (for now).

Help:
- Are they both stubborn and won't admit fault?
- Do they miss each other?
- Do they regret the whole thing?
- Do they hope they can see the person again to explain their side?

BEAT PROMPT 11: "WHAT HAVE I DONE"

The main character realizes they may have made a mistake. This is the memory montage of happy moments that challenge false beliefs.

BEAT PROMPT 11

Help:
- Was the 'dropped shoe' worth throwing away a true connection?
- Was it unforgivable?
- What can they do to mend the situation?
- Was it just a miscommunication?

87

Beat Prompt 12: "I Choose You"

After the moment of realization, the main character chooses love over doubt and fear.

(This is where they have decided to put it all on the line. They decide what they want and will do whatever it takes to get that person. Make sure to answer -how did they get to this place? What are they willing to do?)

BEAT PROMPT 12

Help:

- What happens to make them do this?
- What are they willing to sacrifice?
- What internal demons do they root out?
- How do they decide to follow love and forsake their false beliefs?

89

BEAT PROMPT 13: "BOOM BOX MOMENT" / GRAND GESTURE

Climax/ Sacrifice/ Grand Gesture - Show the main character putting it all on the line. Actions speak louder than words. You must show them making a grand gesture to display overcoming internal and external conflicts and adversity. How do they show their love? Think grand love languages, how do they tell each other of their love and accept it?

BEAT PROMPT 13

Help:
- Do they face a fear to show the other how much they care?
- Do they do something they swore they would never do?
- Have they decided to risk everything for this person?

BEAT PROMPT 14: HAPPILY EVER AFTER (DENOUEMENT)

This is the happy ending we've been working towards. Let us enjoy it! Show them together, happy and safe. Show how they have changed and make sure to resolve their internal and external conflicts fully. Make sure you fulfill expectations, close all arcs, explain all plot holes.

BEAT PROMPT 14

Help:
- What made them both realize they were meant to be together?
- How did they resolve their conflict?
- What makes their relationship work?
- Are loose ends tied up?

BEAT PROMPT 15. EPILOGUE

You can continue the denouement for a further story - Is there a wrench hurled into their world, or it can be 20 years on - where is the happy couple now? Is another couple destined for the same happy fate?

BEAT PROMPT 15

Help:
- Show what happens in the future, has love endured?
- You've done the work to make this a stand alone novel. Could a future conflict lead to a series?

INTENTIONALLY LEFT

Blank

(please use this to doodle or take notes)

Part 4:

TROUBLESHOOTING

For when the words or thoughts just don't come, and you fear your muse is in hermit mode.

- Random diversions for when you get stuck
- Word lists
- Scenario prompts

DIVERSION #1

WRITE ABOUT
THIS COLLAGE.

(CHOOSE ONE
IMAGE OR ALL.)

DIVERSION #2
FILL -IN STORY

It was a _ _ _ _ _ _ and _ _ _ _ _ _
adjective.   adjective.

_ _ _ _ _ _ _ _. _ _ _ _ _ _ _ _ _ _ had just bought a
noun   proper noun

_ _ _ _ _ _ _. _ _ _ thought it was _ _ _ _ _.
noun   pronoun   adjective.

Had it not been for _ _ _ _ _ _ _, _ _ would
noun   pronoun

have _ _ _ _ _ _ _ _. But really who could
verb

have known the truth. Mother, that's
who. Mother had always said, 'the truth
will out'. _ _ _ _ _ _ worried if _ _ _ _ _ _
proper noun   pronoun

would show. _ _ _ heard a whistle and
pronoun

looked to see _ _ _ _ _ _ _ _ _ _ _ _ _ _ at
Proper Noun   verb

_ _ _. They _ _ _ _ _ _ _ and _ _ _ _ _ _.
pronoun   verb   verb

THE END

Diversion #3

Research Suggestions

1. Look up three types of butterflies (or flying insects) in your area.
2. Look up how to identify and describe clouds.
3. Find a funny victorian curse word.
4. Learn about a famous piece of art.
5. Name 20 parts of the body.
6. How many ways can you describe a rump/butt/gluteus/behind...etc.
7. Eye colors and variations (ex. descriptions grey, turqoise, & black).
8. Look up your birthstone/gemstone.
9. What astronomical event is happening near you soon?
10. Look up an emotions wheel.

DIVERSION #4

COLOR AND DOODLE

DIVERSION #5

DESIGN A BOOK COVER

DIVERSION #6

WRITE YOUR DREAM REVIEW FOR YOUR NOVEL

Book Reviews

WORD LIST

add your own words here

graceful

quirky

awkward

regal

illuminated

bright eyed

burning

fluttery

intriguing

spicy

satin

plump

injurious

guilt

snarky

sharp

sentient

spark

WORD LIST

waltz

waggle

wrap

walk

shiver

stroke

shift

shudder

flex

glide

cling

bite

grasp

graze

glance

flee

sway

stretch

SCENARIO PROMPT 1

Character burns dinner, setting the smoke detector off, again...

SCENARIO PROMPT 2

They had always dreamed of traveling, but they hadn't thought
everything through. And now stuck in a foreign country without...

SCENARIO PROMPT 3

Axe throwing-- cool date or traumatic event?

Scenario prompt 4

Lying about being able to cook a souffle had got her into more
trouble than she could have ever imagined.

INTENTIONALLY LEFT

Blank

(please use this to doodle or take notes)

Part 5:

AFTERGLOW

Congratulations!!

You did it!! Please take a moment to congratulate yourself! It does not matter if you filled out everything or not - if you tried - you succeeded in getting your creativity going!

Please take a few minutes to summarize your work in the following pages for the ideas you want to keep and further explore.

We are so proud of you!
Go you!

Intentionally
Left

Blank

(please use this to doodle or take notes)

My Book of Romance

AFTER TAKE
(fill out to easily reference &
keep you on track as you write your draft)

Working Title:

Romantic trope: (please circle one or fill-in)
Enemies to lovers, Friends to Lovers, Secret/Mistaken Identity,
Fake relationship, Love Triangle, Second Chance Romance.
Other_____

Points of View:

Where:

When:

Character 1:

Character 2:

Blurb:
(100-200 words with: Hook, Characters, Tone, Genre, Conflict &
Stakes.)

Summary

What of your work do you want to keep in your emerging storyline?
Or write one sentence for each beat.

SUMMARY

SUMMARY

SUMMARY

SYNOPSIS

Lastly- compress and simplify your summary into a synopsis.

(The boring, factual sales pitch of your story, less than 500 words, but containing the narrative arc, major plot points, and main characters.)

NOTES

Thank
YOU!

FOR BEING YOU!

Made in the USA
Middletown, DE
10 September 2024

60124731R00070